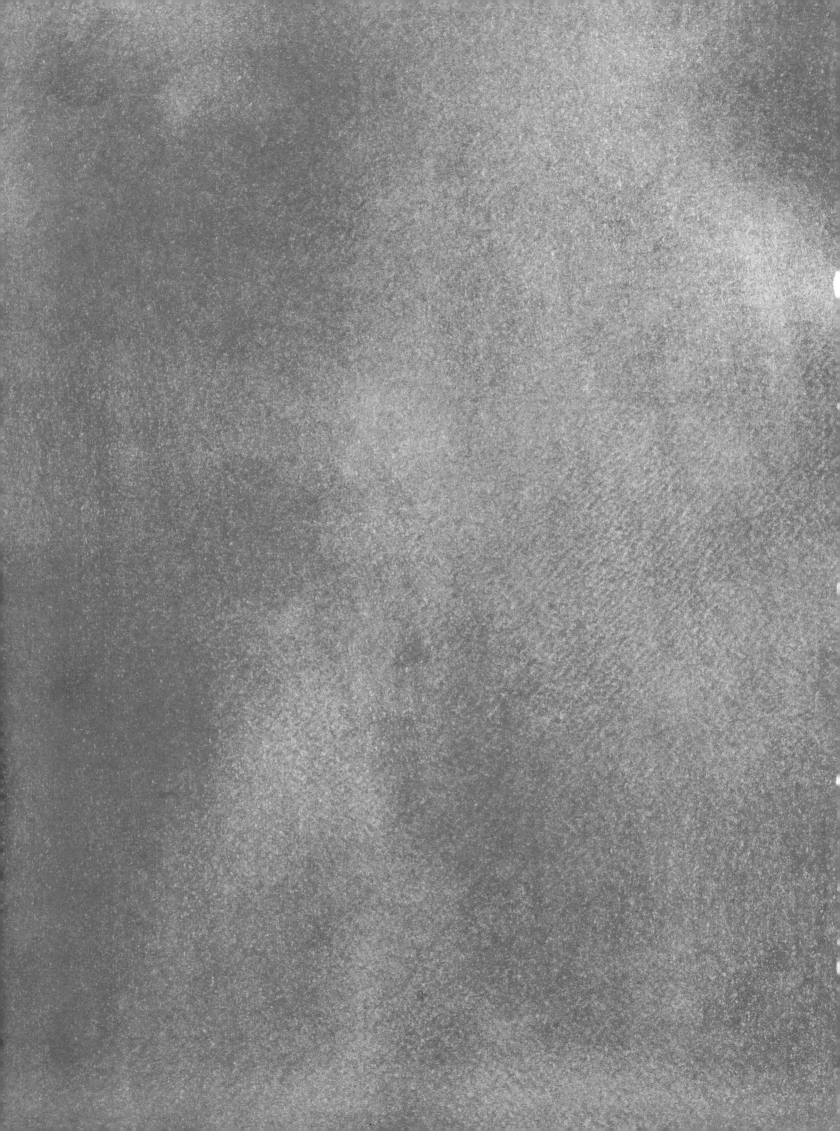

The
BIG
ADVENTURE
of the

SMALLS

Helen Stephens

ALADDIN

New York   London   Toronto   Sydney   New Delhi

To Gerry & Frieda

– H. S.

ALADDIN
An imprint of Simon & Schuster Children's Publishing Division
1230 Avenue of the Americas, New York, NY 10020
First Aladdin hardcover edition May 2012
Text and illustrations copyright © 2012 by Helen Stephens
All rights reserved, including the right of reproduction in whole or in part in any form.
ALADDIN is a trademark of Simon & Schuster, Inc., and related logo
is a registered trademark of Simon & Schuster, Inc.
Original English language edition first published in the UK in 2012 under the title
The Big Adventure of The Smalls by Egmont UK Limited,
239 Kensington High Street, London, W8 6SA.
The author has asserted her moral rights.
For information about special discounts for bulk purchases, please contact
Simon & Schuster Special Sales at 1-866-506-949 or business@simonandschuster.com.
The Simon & Schuster Speakers Bureau can bring authors to your live event.
For more information or to book an event contact the
Simon & Schuster Speakers Bureau at 1-866-248-3049 or
visit our website at www.simonspeakers.com.
Designed by Karina Granda
The text of this book was set in Pastonchi.
Manufactured in Malaysia 1111 PTE
2 4 6 8 10 9 7 5 3 1
This book has been cataloged with the Library of Congress.
ISBN 978-1-4424-5058-8
ISBN 978-1-4424-5069-1 (eBook)

Paul and Sally Small live at Small Hall.

Only Small Hall *isn't* very small . . .

It's **HUGE!**

There are clocks as
TALL as trees,

and plates as
BIG as wheels.

Small
Hall
Summer
Party
jam cakes
soda

And there's always
something *special* going on.

It was an especially special night.

It was the night of
The Small Hall Grand Ball.
Everyone was very busy
getting ready.

But the only thing that
Paul and Sally Small were
getting ready for . . .

was bed.

"Good night, little Smalls," said Mum and Dad.

As they lay listening in the dark,
they could hear the first guests arriving
and the orchestra warming up.

"Come on, Paul," said Sally.
"I want to see."

They crept onto the stairs.
Paul held up his teddy, *Mr. Puddles*,
so he could see the party starting downstairs too.
"He'll fall," warned Sally . . . but it was too late.

Mr. Puddles tumbled through the banister.

"Uh-oh!" cried Paul.

"What shall we do?" said Sally.
"Go, go, go!" said Paul.

So that's exactly what they did.

Whooooosh!

They slid down the banister and landed—**bump**— at the bottom. "Quick," said Sally. "Before anybody sees us!"

They peeped into the
party, looking for
Mr. Puddles.

"The suit of armor
can be our lookout,"
said Sally.
"Come on."

"Can't see *Mr. Puddles* here . . ."

whispered Sally.

"Follow me."

And they
sneaked
through the
corridor toward
a tiny
SECRET
DOOR
hidden in
the wall . . .

up into a secret passageway!

It was **DARK** and **SPOOKY** inside.

Sally shone her flashlight around.
"Uh-oh," said Paul.
"It's all right, it's only a dusty old bear," said Sally.
"Can't see *Mr. Puddles* here. Come on."

They crawled along the passageway until,
finally—out they popped in the kitchen.

Mrs. Goggins, the cook,
was just putting something in the oven.

"Quick,"
said Sally.
"Hide!"

She lifted the lid of
an enormous silver dish.
It was full of cakes.

Paul and Sally had just hopped in
and popped a cake in their
mouths when . . .

the silver dish began to rock and sway. "Uh-oh," said Paul.

The waiter lifted
the lid of the
silver dish,
and Paul
and Sally
darted out . . .

and disguised
themselves as a
vase of flowers . . .

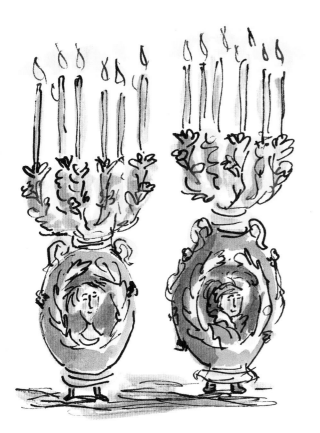

then as a pair
of candelabras.

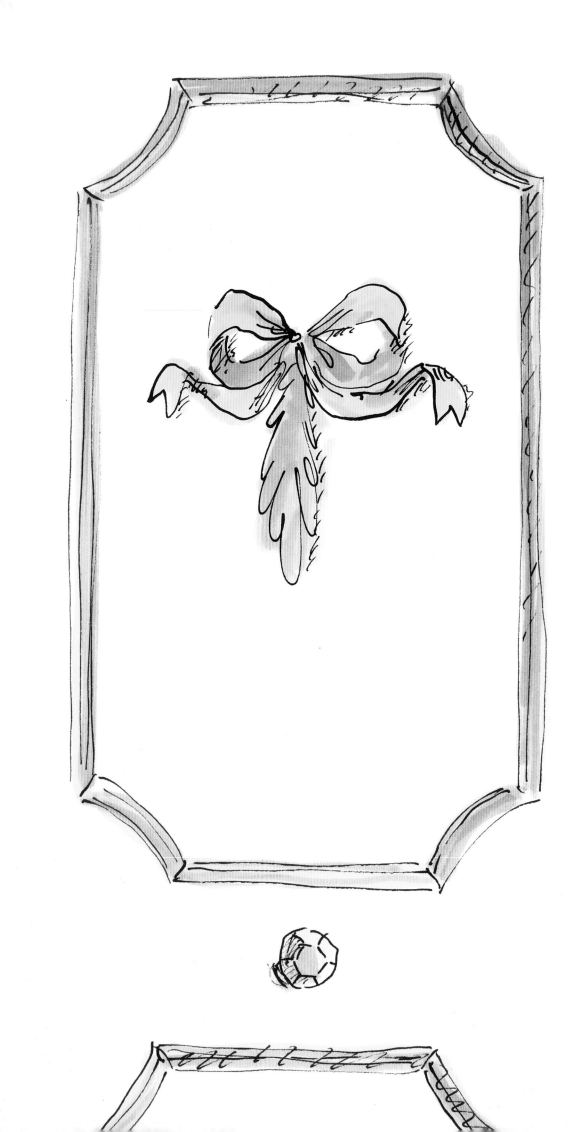

Then,
quick as
a flash,
they
shimmied
up the
statue
to get a
better
view.

"Weeeeeee!"

said Paul.

"I think *Mr. Puddles* is this way!" shouted Sally.

And on the
next swing
they climbed
down the curtains
and hid under a table.

And there was *Mr. Puddles!*

"Lady Pom-Pom!" Sally said.
"Give *Mr. Puddles* back right now!"

Lady Pom-Pom looked at Paul and Sally . . .

then she jumped up and dashed away!

"It's not funny," said Sally,
as they rushed up the stairs.
"Give him back!"

"Uh-oh," said Paul.

Sally and Paul followed
the messy trail right back into . . .

their bedroom.
But where was Lady Pom-Pom **now?**

"Drop!" ordered Paul.

And *Mr. Puddles* fell into his arms.

"Phewww," said Sally.
"We got him back . . .

and nobody even saw."